Am I Ready
For Christmas?

REECE, ARE YOU READY FOR CHRISTMAS? - MOMMY

Published in association with Bear With Us Productions

Am I Ready For Christmas?

WRITTEN BY RAYNA FLOWERS

ILLUSTRATED BY JOHANNA ZVERZINA

BEAR WITH US
PRODUCTIONS

I sat on Dad's lap and could hardly wait to tell him all the things that I wanted.

"I want a transforming car, some play dough, of course. Red, green, yellow... bring me the works! Cars, track, Legos. I need lots and lots of building blocks. More crayons and paper, so I can write to you next year."

"Don't worry about clothes, shoes or books. Daddy and Mommy always buy that stuff."

"But don't forget my robot or my gaming system."

"OK, I'm done.

WAIT!

Video Games.
Now I'm done."

"Wow, you are giving Santa a pretty long list!" said my dad.
"I know, but I'm sure he can handle it."
Every year my dad and I practiced me sitting on Santa's lap.
I wanted to be completely comfortable when the time came.

"I hope so," chuckled my dad,
"but have you upheld your end of the bargain?"
I sat there with a puzzled looked on my face.
"What have you done to deserve those things?" asked Dad.

I sat on the living room floor and thought about my morning.

I jumped up and ran off.
"Be back , Dad!"

"I'm Baacckk!"

I screamed as I slid into the living room. Dad was helping my mom and baby sister hang up Christmas decorations.

Dad looked around and noticed the chores I had completed.

"Thanks for completing your chores, son, but that's not enough for Santa to bring you gifts."

"**What!** I did everything I was supposed to do!"

I couldn't contain my emotions any longer and I started to cry.

"Santa likes people to do things from the goodness of their hearts. Not because they want something in return," said Dad.

I sat on our front porch and sulked. I couldn't believe that in one year all the rules about Santa had changed.

When I looked up, I noticed Mrs. Kelly taking her groceries out of her car. I always helped her with groceries because she lived on the second floor.

"Thank you, young man."

"No problem, Mrs. Kelly."

"I hope Santa brings you all your heart's desires.
Merry Christmas," said Mrs. Kelly.

Under my breath, I mumbled, "I doubt it."
"Merry Christmas to you too, Mrs. Kelly."

While walking out of Mrs. Kelly's building, I noticed a little girl had dropped her blanket.

Without hesitation, I grabbed the blanket off the ground and took off running down the street.

"Thank you, thank you, thank you. This is her favorite blanket. I don't know what I would have done if she would have lost it!" said the little girl's mom.

"No problem at all. My little sister has a favorite blanket too. I completely understand."

As I walked back to my house, a smile formed across my face and I felt warm inside. I did not know why, but I was happy.

I ran to tell my parents how I was feeling, but when I opened the door, I noticed my sister crying.

I continued running towards my room, grabbed all the crayons I could find and placed them right in front of my sister.

"These are for you, princess."
Then I kissed her on the forehead.

"Time to go see Santa!" announced Dad.

On the ride, all I could think about was telling Santa how happy I was. To my surprise, there wasn't a wait. I ran right up to Santa and sat on his lap. Before he could speak , I blurted out,

"Santa, I am so happy!"

"Ho-Ho-Ho. Why is that so, young man?"

I looked at him with a puzzled look on my face. "I don't know. All I did was help Mrs. Kelly with her groceries, return a favorite blanket to a baby and gave my sister my crayons."

"Those sound like great things to be proud about. So, what would you like for Christmas this year?"

I thought long and hard about my answer.

"Santa, for Christmas this year I want to feel this feeling all year round."

"Ho-Ho-H..."

"AND A GAMING SYSTEM!

I would also like a gaming system, please."

"Ho-Ho-Ho. You are the only one that can control your feelings. Remember that. Also, I will talk to the elves regarding the gaming system."

"Ho-Ho-Ho! Merry Christmas, young man!"

Once home, I helped with the last-minute decorations, dressed my sister in her Christmas pajamas and laid out the snacks for Santa and his reindeers. Once in bed, I drifted off to sleep with happy thoughts in my head.

When I woke up the next morning, I still felt happy and warm inside and I genuinely believed I was ready for Christmas.

Merry Christmas!

The End

Rayna Flowers

Rayna lives in New Jersey with her son Reece, A.K.A. Chewy Rodriquez. During the day you can find them watching Blaze and the Monster Machines, engaging in arts and crafts, hunting for their next bedtime story or simply enjoying a day at the park. Rayna is also the author of the story/coloring book ZOO-A-PALOOZA.

You can follow their journey on Instagram & Facebook: Lyfewithus.18

f @Lyfewithus.18

⊙ @Lyfewithus.18

Made in the USA
Monee, IL
14 November 2021

82106407R00021